LOST IN A DARK FOREST

BY
SANDRA JAY KINSLOW

Sandra Jay Kinslow

PublishAmerica
Baltimore

© 2004 by Sandra Jay Kinslow.

All rights reserved. No part of this book may be reproduced, stored in a retrieval system or transmitted in any form or by any means without the prior written permission of the publishers, except by a reviewer who may quote brief passages in a review to be printed in a newspaper, magazine or journal.

First printing

ISBN: 1-4137-1817-5
PUBLISHED BY PUBLISHAMERICA BOOK PUBLISHERS
www.publishamerica.com
Baltimore

Printed in the United States of America

In Appreciation
To
Nelda Adams & Phyllis Adams
For the editing and grammar work done on
Lost In A Dark Forest. Thank you both.

Chapter 1

While many were enjoying the lights of the Christmas tree and ornaments and decorations that were placed carefully around the house, Janelle was trying to find a way out of this dark forest. It was hard to see the brightly lit up Christmas trees, because of all the other dark trees in this dark forest that surrounded her. She smiled at people and went through the motions of the holidays, but just couldn't find the laughter within her that reflected a happy heart. Most of the streets had houses all decorated for the season and were pretty to look at. All she saw was darkness and gloom, as she would drive down the streets. When she was with others she would remark about how the pretty Christmas lights were, and the beauty of the homes she saw, but in her heart she saw nothing but dark streets, empty houses, and broken families. It was so hard to get into the spirit of things.

Janelle wrapped packages for the family, which she had carefully shopped for that year. Buying gifts had been tough, and not something she had enjoyed. She loved her family though and was hopeful the grandkids would enjoy the gifts she had selected for them. She had hung red ribbons on the doors to make things look more festive. She put up the Christmas tree, and decorated it with ornaments she had made over the years. Lights were hung on the tree and sparkled when she plugged them in.

Janelle baked, sewed, made things and decorated the house where it reflected the beauty of the holiday. Each day she kept hoping she would find an opening in this dark forest of grief and loneliness. She could only hope things would be okay when Christmas Day arrived. She wanted this to be a good Christmas for the sake of the kids and her precious grandchildren. She knew they were missing their dad and grandpa.

The kids came with their families on Christmas Eve and the laughter from the children seemed to reach into her troubled and sad heart. She enjoyed the time with them and seeing their eyes full of delight when they would open something they really wanted or liked.

In spite of her efforts to be happy that day, her kids, who are all grown up now and have children of their own, seemed to sense Mom was just having a rough time of it and did their best to be cheerful while dealing with their own loss, their dad they loved. We hugged and held each other and smiled and did our best to make the first Christmas after his death a Christmas of joy in spite of the loss. Janelle, despite her heavy heart, seemed to make it through the darkness that Christmas Eve with family. The family left early that evening to go to their own homes to prepare for the big day, Christmas Day.

After the family left, she closed the door behind them and sat down and cried. She was exhausted from trying to be so brave for everyone, while she walked around in this deep, dark forest of pain and loss. She only wanted to find a glimmer of light somewhere that would bring her out of this forest of gloom, tears and sadness. Instead of being with everyone the next day on Christmas Day, she wished she could just stay in bed and not go anywhere. It just seemed to be too much to have to go and put on a front for others and pretend she was doing okay, when she knew she wasn't okay. She didn't want to spoil the happiness for others by breaking down and crying. She knew the kids and James' family would be expecting her to join them for Christmas. They didn't want her to be alone on Christmas, but she was alone even when she was with her children, grandchildren, family and friends, because James wasn't there with her. She had hoped that having everyone at the house on Christmas Eve would be enough to help her get through the holidays, but instead it was a reminder of how very much her life had changed since James' death, and she felt lonely and miserable on this Christmas Eve night and deeply troubled by the loss of the dearest person in the world to her. He was her husband of more than 36 years, a man that she loved more than words could describe. He was her best friend, sweetheart, one and only true love. They had met when she was only 15 years old. She had married him when she turned 18 years old, and they had been through some difficult times during their marriage because of his sickness. Most of the 36 years they had been married, he had been in and out of hospitals and through multiple operations. In

LOST IN A DARK FOREST

spite of the sickness, it seemed with each passing year, their love had grown much deeper and they were so much in love. He had become her whole world. Despite his sickness he had always been a good husband, kind, caring and so supportive of her. He hated her having to take care of him because he was sick and disabled. He hated not being able to work. He wanted to take care of his family instead of them having to take care of him.

James suffered multiple health problems. Many years of sickness and disabilities left him needing lots of tender loving care. He had two brain operations for ruptured cerebral aneurisms that required a lot of medical care during his last 12 years of life. She was devoted to his care and so happy she could be there for him. She did her best to meet his daily needs with love and devotion. They shared a love that many dream of, wish for, and few find. They were among the fortunate few that truly find their soul mates. This is a person you truly love, who in return loves you totally and completely.

Some are unable to cope with being told they are facing a terminal illness, and might not live long. Janelle knew her husband had faced the ugly monster of death with an unbelievable courage. He never stopped fighting to live until he drew his last breath.

Years prior to his death he had faced those brain operations, which were both life and death situations, with such courage. James had been told that he had four aneurisms in the brain. Two were in locations in the brains that could't be operated on. If one of those two remaining aneurisms that could't be repaired by surgery ruptured, nothing could have been done to save him. He would have died shortly after the rupture.

He also had aneurisms on his main aorta, which is one of the main blood vessels in the body, and you can die within five minutes of a rupture of the aorta if you are unable to get medical help right away. James had over 35 medical problems, most of which were severe. He dealt with these daily in those last years of his life. Despite all of these problems, he continued to live each day with such faith in God and never once gave up or became bitter because of his problems.

He knew life was precious and he lived each day as if it was his last day on earth. To stand up, sit up in a chair or even sit up in bed was impossible because he would pass out from his blood pressure fluctuating so much. He was forced to lie in bed all the time. He also had problems with all the automatic functions of your body, like your heart, bowels, bladder, lungs, and other functions, like breathing. The first brain operation from the rupture of aneurisms and pooling of blood in the back of the brain had caused him to have a stroke. The second operation caused him to lose all of his communication skills. He was unable to write, speak or communicate with anyone. With a year of therapy, in which he was told he would never be able to regain any of his communication skills, he proved them wrong and regained almost 70% of his speech loss. He never got bitter or became excessively angry, even though he had enough wrong with him to make him angry and bitter. Watching James having to deal with his problems daily, and doing so with such courage, had given her the courage also to keep going.

Many, if they had been in James' condition, would have rejected care and become bitter and frustrated if they had been forced to face the things that he had dealt with each day he lived. Some people who are unable to cope with terminal illness can often be found in this dark forest that Janelle had found herself in after James' death.

Being told you are going to die is not an easy thing to deal with. Watching the man she loved so much deal with his problems daily, doing so with such love for everyone and always just saying, "Oh well," and not sinking into despair or depression had given Janelle the strength she had needed to care for him day and night. His death had come slowly, day by day, as his body began to wear out and the problems became more severe and medically un-treatable.

She thought of the times the doctors had shaken their head in amazement that James was still alive and he hadn't given up. The physicians had given him the best care anyone could possibly receive.

Nurses and Home Health personnel who had come to their home were amazed at how he would always smile at them and tell them everything would be all right. He had inspired everyone with his courage, loving smiles, his love for everyone, and his personality. He had been a patient they always looked forward to seeing and taking care of.

He had kept his heart and mind focused on God. Janelle was grateful that her dad, who was a minister, and had been visiting with them prior to the time of James' death, had read him the scriptures in PSALMS 23: 1-6 shortly before he died. *"The Lord is my Shepherd; I shall not want. He maketh me to lie down in green pastures: he leadeth me beside the still waters. He restoreth my soul: He leadeth me in the paths of righteousness for his name's sake. Yea, though I walk through the valley of the shadow of death, I will fear no evil: for thou art with me; thy rod and thy staff they comfort me. Thou preparest a table before me in the presence of mine enemies: thou anointest my head with oil: my cup runneth over. Surely goodness and mercy shall follow me all the days of my life: and I will dwell in the house of the Lord forever."* James lived by those words and he knew that God would be with him as he walked through the valley of the shadow of death. While he waited patiently for God to call him home, he had allowed Janelle to do whatever she could to make him comfortable and to provide care for him. He had never complained or objected to whatever decision was made to give him the best care possible. He had known in the end it wouldn't help much, but he had apparently known that everyone needed to feel they had done all they could for him. As he had watched them care for him, he had seen the pleasure it had given each one in trying to make him more comfortable while he waited for God to call him home.

He had kept his eyes on God, knowing that some day soon the angels of God would come and carry him over that great gulf, and into the kingdom of God.

Psalms 130:5 *"I wait for the Lord, my soul doth wait, and in his word do I hope."*

Psalms 91:11 *"For he shall give his angels charge over thee, to keep thee in all thy ways."*

Janelle's mind kept going back to the time prior to his death when the doctors had come to her with decisions that had needed to be made regarding his condition. They told her there was no hope for him to survive this time, and that the things that were being done up to this point were only prolonging the inevitable. Having fought by his side all those years to help him survive the many medical problems that he had

SANDRA JAY KINSLOW

been confronted with, it was heartbreaking to know that the fighting was over. There was nothing more anyone could do. The doctors, medical staff and other medical personnel had done all they could to help him. Even the antibiotics that had been used to try to control the pseudomonas infections were no longer working and doing more harm than good. It was time to remove the medication. It was hard for her to believe there had been no options left, that he would die soon and nothing more could be done but stand by and watch. Time had been spent in prayer, seeking strength from God to face what she had known in her heart was God's will, to release this man of his suffering so he could receive his Heavenly reward. This can only be accomplished when you die the physical death, so that spiritually you can live forever with God.

She had watched James lying there in his hospital bed at the point of death, knowing that he was fighting to live because he loved everyone so much and did not want to leave them, yet knowing that if he let go and allowed God to have his way, he would be liberated from this life, freed of the suffering.

Psalms 73: 26 *"My flesh and my heart faileth: but God is the strength of my heart and my portion forever."*

She had known it was not fair to expect him to continue to endure all he had been through just for her. To try to keep him alive when he was in a coma and had no chance to make it so everyone could have him here on earth a few more hours would have been cruel. She sat in tears as she remembered that night and knew that it was time to let God's will be done. The doctor agreed with the family decision and James' wishes to not be coded and gave James medication to ease his suffering as Janelle and those that loved him stood by with their love and prayers. Janelle had known when his time was almost up. She had watched him as his breathing had changed, and knew in her heart that God would be taking him soon. As she continued to remember the night of James' death, she recalled how heavy her heart had felt knowing that she was seeing him alive for the last time.

James had been in a coma and could not tell them bye, but she knew he would be going to Heaven. They had talked about what Heaven

LOST IN A DARK FOREST

would be like, and both agreed that should something ha~~p~~ them, the other one would join them in Heaven someday. both been Christians most of their lives. He had also asked h~~e~~ put him on life support if he was ever in a vegetative state, and s~~h~~ agreed to honor his wishes. He had wanted her out of love for him, let him go if he was ever in that state, and just allow God to take him home to Heaven when it was his time to die. Remembering all of this now was so painful, yet when the time had come, she had honored his wishes. She had known it was time to let him go.

Janelle remembered like it was yesterday, walking up to his bed. She had taken a comb and combed his beautiful white hair. He always liked for his hair to look nice. She had held his hand in her one hand, while she had stroked his face and spoke softly to him. He seemed to have heard her, because as she spoke, her voice had seemed to comfort him that day as it had done many times in the past when he would be in so much pain. She had told him, the last time he would ever hear her voice, how much she loved him and always would. She had known by his breathing and the things that the doctor had told her that the angels would be coming soon to take him home to Heaven. Janelle had reminded him to not be afraid, that she was there by his side, and that for the two of them it would not be good-bye, because she would see him in just a little while. The nurse told her later that those words had given James assurance and permission to go be with God, knowing he would be seeing her again, because after she had spoken those words, he drew his last breath. James had died that night and had left his pain and suffering behind and had gone to be with God. He had shed his earthly body and now had a heavenly body and was up in Heaven, enjoying the beauty and rewards of his Heavenly home.

John 5:24 *"Verily, verily I say unto you, He that hearth my word, and believeth on him that sent me, hath everlasting life, and shall not come into condemnation; but is passed from death unto life."*

John 8:51 *"Verily, verily I say unto you, If a man keep my saying, he shall never see death."*

SANDRA JAY KINSLOW

After so many years of poor health, God said enough was enough of his suffering and pain and the angels of God took him home to Heaven. In her mind she knew that her husband was so much better off up in Heaven with God. There were no feelings of guilt or remorse over the care that had been given to him, but her heart said to lose him was just too much.

She hadn't minded the long hours of care given to him, loss of sleep, or social life, or that she couldn't go shopping or visiting friends or family. He had needed her constant care, and Janelle, as she lay there sobbing, thought of all of the love and care he had needed and knew she had done everything for him that she could and now he was gone.

During those many years of caring for him, she had prayed and asked God to give her strength to keep going when she would feel herself wearing down and in need of renewed strength. God answered her prayers and gave the strength needed to the very night James had died. He also gave Janelle the strength needed to hold up the last two weeks, when James was in the hospital and expected to die at any time. God's strength could be felt during the funeral, and during the weeks that followed. She didn't grieve over his death, she grieved over her loss. She was alone now and there was no one there that night to lie next to in her bed. Her sweetheart was no longer there by her side. She knew she would never see his face again, and she rolled over, soaked her pillow with her tears and sorrow in her heart. It was so painful having to let go of him. He was no longer in pain and suffering, but she was in pain, a horrible pain she couldn't even describe. She had never known a pain like this before in her life. She knew God said in His word that He would be there for her and yet as she lay in her bed that night, all alone and hurting, she wondered why she could not seem to feel his presence.

He was up in Heaven now, where he could walk, talk, and is free of the limitations that had plagued him here on earth.

Revelations 21:4 *"And God shall wipe away all tears from their eyes: and there shall be no more death, neither sorrow, nor crying, neither shall there be any more pain: for the former things are passed away."*

LOST IN A DARK FOREST

Isaiah 14:3 *"And it shall come to pass in the day that the Lord shall give thee rest from thy sorrow, and from thy fear, and from the hard bondage within thou wast made to serve."*

Each day Janelle saw or experienced little things that remind her of her loss and scriptures that reminded her of his gain. It had not been easy to adjust to life without him.

John 16:32 *"Behold, the hour cometh, yea, is now come, that ye shall be scattered, every man to his own, and shall leave me alone: and yet I am not alone, because the Father is with me."*

Everywhere she turned there were little reminders of his absence. She struggled from day to day, seeking strength, comfort and help from God. Her forest seemed darkest at night and she often cried herself to sleep out of loneliness and a sense of emptiness now that he was gone. She missed having him there by her side to talk to and share things with.

Christmas Eve night she had found it difficult to sleep. She reflected back on James and all they had been through during their many years together. She loved him so much and missed him more than words could say. She knew she had to find the courage within herself to move on with her life and face his death, and her loss. She cried and prayed, asking God to help her just get through the night. She realized God had been there for her in the past and had given her strength right up to the day James had died.

Now she felt totally exhausted and worn out. It seemed to almost take too much strength to even breathe. She dreaded the next day and wished she could sleep, but all she could think about was James and how much she missed him. She knew in her heart she must depend on God completely to survive all that had happened. She knew she had to learn how to adjust to life without her sweetheart.

Sometime during the wee hours of the morning, Janelle finally went to sleep that Christmas Eve. She woke up the next morning, feeling as if James' death had taken her from life to death. It felt like 98% of her had died also. She felt as if she had gone from daylight to darkness overnight. It was like someone had blindfolded her, knocked her out and when she awoke she was in this dark forest. Nothing seemed right to her, and even though she knew she was still alive, it almost seemed like it was too much effort to even try to keep going. In her heart she knew she was very much alive, yet aware that if she had died when James did, she wouldn't be here feeling all of this pain and such feelings of gloom and misery. There were no thoughts of suicide, just an awareness of her pain and loss. If God chose to take her at that moment, she would have been more than ready to leave this world of pain and suffering and the thoughts of Heaven, and James being there with all the beauty and joy of Heaven, made her envy James being there without her. The scriptures had revealed to her that there is no sickness, sorrow, pain, suffering and no tears in Heaven.

Revelations 21:4 *"And God shall wipe away all tears from their eyes; and there shall be no more death, neither sorrow, nor crying, neither shall there be any more pain: for the former things are passed away."*

As she continued to reflect back upon the days prior to his funeral, she remembered feeling so numb. When it had come time to view him in the casket, she felt as if her heart could not stand the pain inside her. It was worse than anything she could have ever imagined.

Janelle remembered a dream she had when James had been real sick. In her dream James had died and she was viewing him in the casket and she had awakened with tears in her eyes. She had been so relieved to see him lying there next to her, sleeping and okay. The dream stuck in her mind and she wondered if this was how she would feel when James passed from this life to be with God.

When James died, and Janelle saw him at the funeral home, lying in his casket, she had felt that same horrible pain she had experienced in the dream. This time though it was not a dream, and the pain so much worse, because James was not going to wake up in the morning next to her in bed. He had gone to be with God. Having to say good-bye to him, knowing she would never see his earthly body again, had been the hardest things she had ever had to do. She knew she would see him again in Heaven, but for now she had to deal with living in this world without him.

LOST IN A DARK FOREST

The days since his death were often just a blur. She would forget things and go somewhere and not remember how she even got there. Her whole body was totally exhausted and it took all her energy just to put one foot in front of the other.

The past three months since his death seemed unreal and like some kind of dream she would wake up from like she had done before and he would be there next to her and everything would be okay. Day by day though she realized that this was no dream, this was reality, and he was gone and he wouldn't be back. The thoughts of that were almost too much to even think about. The tears came often. The lump in her throat made things difficult to swallow. James was dead, and she knew she had to accept this.

She almost envied him being with God while she remained here on earth feeling as if life had left her too, yet still very much alive. It was no wonder that some people resorted to taking their own life because of the pain, feeling of emptiness and wondering what was left that was worth living for. She knew that wasn't the answer. God had left her here for a reason and had a purpose in mind for her. She just longed for ease from the pain and a way of escape from the forest of agony and despair.

As she tried to eat her breakfast that Christmas morning she felt frightened as she realized she had no sense of direction in her life. She was unsure of everything, where to go, or what to do. These were just some of the many feelings of uneasiness for her. She knew from her years of serving God that He was there for her and all she had to do was seek Him, yet this Christmas morning she had trouble even feeling His presence. She felt out of control. This was a very troubling feeling after so many years of taking care of everything and always being in control.

Now the very things that were once so familiar to her were no longer recognizable. Everything she saw appeared the same to her. Her life had become this forest of trees that all had limbs, which appeared to have the same dark green leaves.

A tree in sunlight that offered shade would be a thing of beauty, but in her dark forest these same trees were ominous and frightening. It was as if its limbs were reaching down holding her next to the ground. They seemed to smother her and kept the light from penetrating through the darkness of her forest. These same limbs filled with leaves would have been a welcome retreat from the brightness of the sunshine outside of her forest, but in her forest of grief, they were all ugly trees.

As a child she found trees to be a wonderful place to lie beneath and rest. In this horrible forest of darkness there could be found no rest for her, just darkness and sadness.

As she sat sipping her coffee Christmas morning, her first Christmas without James, she sat listening for a sound or a glimmer of light that might help give her a sense of direction in this dark forest she lived in now. She felt so lost in this forest and so alone as she sat quietly. All she could hear were the sounds of her own heart beating fast as she grew more frightened by the darkness around her. Instead of seeing the beauty of Christmas she could only see the darkness of this Christmas. A Christmas tree was sitting in her home, but she was unable to see it in her mind, even though her eyes could see it clearly. She only saw the forest and the darkness from the trees that surrounded her. Christmas, she knew, would pass, and then would come spring.

Lost in this world of grief, she wondered if she would ever be able to hear the birds in the springtime? The birds had always been such a joy to her. She loved hearing them sing. Where were the sounds of the squirrels and crickets and other small creatures that had always delighted her with the cute sounds they made?

Nothing seemed to be stirring in the forest of gloom, as she sat frightened like a child wishing its mama or daddy would come and rescue her. Would she be forever deaf to the sounds around her and blind to the beauty of things created by God?

James' death had taken the very warmth out of her body. She felt as cold inside as he felt to her touch when she had kissed him good-bye for the last time as he lay in his coffin. She sat cold and alone that morning in this gloomy forest, hearing no sounds, and cried softly.

For many people, the rising of the sun would bring the welcome of a new day. There would be lots of things to do and places to go and work that must be finished. Life would be exciting for them and worth the routines of each day. Morning for her had just brought continued darkness. The sun would be shining but would go unnoticed. The day's routine would be for many a hectic day, yet for her it was an unsettling day with nothing in mind but to try to escape the darkness that death

LOST IN A DARK FOREST

had brought into her life.

Each day meant trying again to move forward with the hopes that each step would bring her closer to the path that would lead her back to life, sunlight, and the joy of living. Some days the path seemed to not be as dark, and she felt that perhaps it might be bringing her closer to the light that can be found at the edge of the forest.

Luke 1:79 *"To give light to them that sit in darkness and in the shadow of death, to guide our feet into the way of peace."*

There were days when it felt as if she was only walking deeper into the forest. Those were very discouraging days. It was enough to make Janelle wonder why she even bothered to escape, but she was growing tired of the darkness, the density of the forest, and longed for the warmth of sunlight. Each day she made the effort to find life again and would get up and once again go in search of a way to escape this ugly forest of depression and despair. This was a strange feeling being so depressed, considering she had never known depression in her lifetime, and had worked hard to make sure things in life didn't get the best of her. She felt with God on her side she could make it through anything. Yet here she sat, feeling depressed and all alone. In her heart she knew God was there, yet the death of her loved one had somehow thrown her into a depression that she had never expected. This was a natural depression that often occurs when someone dies. She had not expected or been prepared for this and she felt out of control and unable to pull herself out of this depressed state. She called out to God, but it was like this dreadful forest prevented her from reaching God.

Limbs from the trees all around her seem to slap at Janelle in this darkness as she tried to move forward. The brush which had grown beneath the trees seemed to block her from going straight ahead, and she found herself groping for another route, another way around the bushes that acted as barriers. There just didn't seem to be a way of escaping the pains of death, but she was hopeful she would be able to find a way out of this forest of death and it would bring some relief from the pain she felt inside. She was learning that you just can't give up, you have to keep moving, one step at a time. She knew in her heart she had to fight this natural depression or she would be forever lost in this forest of death and forever lost in the past, unable to go on with life as God meant for it to be. As she wandered around in the density of the trees and brushes, searching for life again, she knew she would also have to learn how to deal with this loneliness and emptiness. Life would never be the same, but someway, somehow, she had to find a way to live again and find meaning again in her life.

The scriptures teach you in Psalms 23 that God will be with you through the valleys and shadows of death. You wonder if those scriptures are for those who die a physical death, or could it also be for those that are wandering around the valley of the shadow of death of a loved one?

While searching for answers, she found time to think about the scriptures and to pray. There are many who are lost in the forests who do not know God or how to pray. For her prayers came easily, but sometimes her faith would falter as she sought relief from the pain and loneliness and looked for an escape. When the escape didn't come right away, she would question where God was and wonder if He was even listening to her pleas for His help. Doubts would linger in her mind as she would kneel and beat her fist against the earth, sobbing, and seeking relief from the gripping pain within her.

To be forced to accept the loss of the one you love is not easy, but she knew she must learn to accept this. Death can be good for the person who died, especially when they had endured a lot of sickness. It can be hard to accept or understand when that loved one was healthy and seemed to be in the prime of their life.

As a child of God you know that God always does what is right and best for everyone, and will permit or allow events to happen in this life because that is what is best. God knows what the future holds for each one and Janelle knew He knew what was best for James, but why such pain and suffering after he was gone, had left her wishing more than once that she could have died also.

As a Christian she felt guilty and ashamed of her lack of faith and all her doubts. Had she become, like Thomas the disciple, "doubting Thomas"? Janelle tried to reason with herself and kept telling herself that all of these difficult times would just make her stronger. Then the sorrow she felt would overwhelm her and she questioned how something this bad could possibly make you feel better or stronger.

LOST IN A DARK FOREST

Trees are known for being sturdy and enduring, and Janelle longed to be strong, sturdy and stable once again. As she looked up into the darkness of the trees and tried to see the outline of the limbs, things were blurred from the darkness around her. Attempts to see into the darkness and refocus her eyes were limited. She almost envied the animals their ability to see in darkness. As she strained her eyes, trying to see ahead of her, she kept wondering if she would ever be strong like the tree limbs with their strength and stability. Would she walk again in strong faith, even in the darkness of the forest, or would she continue to question God and wander forever in this forest of grief and disbelief?

As the days and nights passed, she was frightened by the realization that her husband was no longer there to protect her. He had been her protector all those years, and she had always felt nothing would harm her as long as he was here. She knew he would have risen from his deathbed with whatever strength he could muster to come to her defense if he had felt she was threatened. This had given her security and she wasn't afraid. Now he was gone, and she felt so alone and frightened. She knew in her heart though that God could give her spiritual comfort and protection if she would just trust and believe in this promise.

She prayed again in such anguish and then sat quietly, listening and hoping that God would speak to her in a voice that she could hear. She just wanted His assurance that she wasn't alone and that He was there even though she couldn't physically touch or feel Him. Sometimes God doesn't answers you the way you expect. God doesn't always speak to you in a loud voice, sometimes it's a whisper.

I Kings 19:12 *"After the earthquake came a fire, but the Lord was not in the fire. And after the fire came a still, small voice."*

God doesn't always answer you right away when you pray and that can often cause many to doubt that He even hears them. Janelle had been filled with such doubts, but she prayed that God would answer her prayers, but she knew she must ask in faith, believing that He would answer her prayers.

Psalms 66:19-20 *"But verily God hath heard me; he hath attended to the voice of my prayer. Blessed be God, which hath not turned away my prayer, nor his mercy from me."*

With so much time to think about things, Janelle thought of how long James had been sick. In fact, he had been sick off and on most of their marriage. He had been forced to accept early disability retirement due to multiple injuries sustained where he had been employed. This had forced him into an early retirement, so their children never remembered Daddy ever going to work. He had always been there at home.

The fact they were together constantly made his death difficult for Janelle to accept, even though she knew it was best for him. She thought those years of watching him slowly die would prepare her for his inevitable death. When the time came, she found she wasn't really prepared. It had given them time to talk about the future and what he hoped she would do when he was gone, and what would happen if she should die first. There had been time to make prior arrangements for his funeral with the help of her brother, who had previously owned a funeral home and was able to guide her in making her selections and the necessary arrangements. Business matters were taken care of prior to his death, because there had been time to plan ahead. Janelle thought it would be much easier to accept his death, because she had been given time to prepare. She was not prepared for what the death of a loved one is really like. Watching someone slowly slipping away from you due to health problems is within itself a difficult thing to handle. On occasions, Janelle remembered having to go outside and have a good cry so that he was not aware of her pain, especially since he could not stand to see her cry. After a good cry and a talk with God she had got a good grip on herself and had gone back inside to do everything she could for him to make his life as full and complete as possible before he died.

She knew her despair after his death did not stem from feelings of guilt. Her forest of gloom had no feelings of guilt because of what should have been done. She knew in her heart that she had done all she could to help him in every way—emotionally, physically and spiritually. Some people, unfortunately, never leave the darkness because of their feelings of guilt and regrets. For her it was the

LOST IN A DARK FOREST

emptiness, loneliness and frustrations of not having him with her anymore. Her very existence each day had revolved around his care and then suddenly the time came and he wasn't there. Her world had changed so drastically, and she was at a loss as to what to do next. Because of this depressed state of mind, from grieving, she found it difficult to even think about plans for the day or if it even mattered if she even planned anything at all.

It would have been just as easy to have stopped doing anything and simply go through the motions of the day with no plans, no particular thoughts, or concerns. Janelle began to sense that she was giving in to these feelings of depression more and more with each passing day and would sink deeper in despair. Seeing what depression had done to the lives of people she knew, she felt she must fight for all that was within her and allow God to help her or she would never recover from mourning the loss of her loved one. Help was all around her, but unless she was willing to reach out to God and to those around her who were wanting to help her, she would live forever in the past, in this forest of darkness and depression, and forever live in the darkness of death.

The deeper the depression the darker the world is around you. Your days are shadowed by the very darkness that engulfs you.

I Timothy 5:5 *"Now she that is a widow indeed, and desolate, trusteth in God, and continueth in supplications and prayers night and day."*

Does the pain ever go away? She asked this question to some who had lost their loved ones and had experienced such pain. Each one said, "No, but it does get easier." Each one expressed different ways in which the death had affected them. Some said, "The pain is always there, you just learn how to move on with life in spite of the pain and each day it gets easier to deal with the loss." One of her friends told her that life doesn't give you much choice but to accept the fact that you must go on with your life in spite of the loss. That to refuse to accept such a fact will leave you forever in the forest of loneliness, despair and emptiness. Each and every person had to deal with their loss in their own way.

Matthew 4:16 *"The people which sat in darkness saw great light; and to them which sat in the region and shadow of death light is sprung up."*

There was hope and a way out of the forest. Janelle knew she must never give up searching for her way out of this forest of death and despair into the sunlight of love and hope. She often got discouraged when she could almost feel the warmth of the sunshine and see the glimmers of sunlight streaming in through the trees, and then suddenly without warning, something would happen that would send her reeling with pain over some thought, action or the sight of something that brought back memories of the one she had lost.

For Janelle, the first year after James' death had been a lot of going forward and sliding back. She understood why some people stop trying. Many do not know God personally as their Savior. He could be there to help them move forward if they knew Him and would call on Him. Some do not have loved ones and friends to encourage and shout messages of hope and love to them while they are buried in sorrow and grief.

Would she survive? Yes, because she had God there to help her, even when she had been filled with doubts and lack of faith. God hadn't turned His back on her, and His constant abiding love and the Holy Spirit had been there to comfort her. All Janelle had to do was trust God and let Him help her, guide her, heal her broken heart and bind up her wounds.

Psalms 147:3 *"He healeth the broken in heart, and bindeth up their wounds."*

Many won't make it out of their depression and will spend the rest of life on earth in pain and misery. They will be here among us, but barely functioning as human beings. Their lives will be empty and meaningless. Some will never know the joy of love and being loved ever again. Janelle could not imagine her life without God's love. Having been loved all her life, with His love, the love of her deceased husband, and that of family, children, and friends, she longed for a return to a world in which she could not only receive love but also feel

LOST IN A DARK FOREST

alive and want to love in return.

The darkness of death that occurs in this life can become a blessing when you know the one who passed away is a child of God.

> Hebrews 9:15 *"And for this cause he is the mediator of the new testament, that by means of death, for the redemption of the transgressions that were under the first testament, they which are called might receive the promise of eternal inheritance."*

James was a child of God and received his just inheritance. Janelle found joy in knowing that someday they would see each other again in Heaven. She thought of the ones who must say good-bye to their loved ones, knowing they will never see that loved one again.

> Romans 8:16-17 *"The Spirit itself beareth witness with out spirit, that we are the children of God: And if children, then heirs; with Christ: if so be that we suffer with him, that we may be also glorified together."*

Without that assurance Janelle's last hours and time with James would have been even more painful knowing they would never be together again. She thought of her last words to him, 'This is not good-bye, this is *and I will see you in a little while.*' He drew his last breath after those words, and she knew from God's word that she would see James again when her time came to leave this world to join him in Heaven.

> Romans 6:23 *"For the wages of sin is death; but the gift of God is eternal life through Jesus Christ our Lord."*

When Janelle could feel the sting of death so deeply upon her, she just reminded herself that she would see him again soon. She also remembered the suffering he endured when he was alive, and now he no longer suffered the pain and anguish he endured while he was here on earth. She did not wish him back to suffer more, but couldn't help missing him more than words could possibly describe. Is it selfish to have loved your loved one so much that a part of you wishes they had never had to leave you?

When you have loved someone with all your heart, mind and soul, you might feel abandoned and all alone. After their death, you may wish their health could have been better so maybe they wouldn't have had to leave you so soon or you could have done things differently and then perhaps that would have prevented the death.

At times like this many people who have lost loved ones due to an accident will often wonder if they had made different decisions would that have prevented the accident. It is normal to feel this way, but second-guessing doesn't really help much. Most likely nothing you did, or might be able to have done, would have made any difference in most situations. It is appointed unto man a time to die, and only God knows when it's the right time.

Ecclesiastes 3:2 *"A time to be born, and a time to die; a time to plant, and a time to pluck up that which is planted."*

God made the decision as to when it was the right time for her husband, and nothing Janelle did or could have done would have prevented his death. Everything man could do had been done. God decided that a child of His had endured enough in this life and it had been his time for him to reap the rewards of his labor and faithfulness to God while here on earth. God promised in His word He would not put more on you than you could bear. That is why He knows when it's the right time to call a child of His home to be with Him in Heaven. God knows when they have suffered enough.

Philippians 2:27 *"For indeed he was sick nigh unto death: but God had mercy on him; and not on him only, but on me also, lest I should have sorrow upon sorrow."*

Taking care of the car, yard, house, and bills had been things she had to do alone now. Decisions were hers alone to make. She no longer had a husband there to seek his advice on whatever the problem or need might be at the time. James had been so knowledgeable about so many things and she missed having him there with her and having someone to turn to.

Her home had become a darkened forest. She looked around the

LOST IN A DARK FOREST

house, and there were his photos everywhere and little mementos. He had a huge Avon collection that had been displayed on shelves. A neighbor had come when James was so sick and helped her put up the shelves so that he could enjoy viewing the collection while he had lain in his hospital bed. There were lots of other reminders of him all throughout the house. Most of all, she had all of her memories of him and the years they had shared together.

Sometimes she wished she could just hold him one more time, or feel his touch, or hear his voice. The last words he had spoken directly to her just before he went into a coma were 'I love you.' She could hear those words now as she looked around her and remembered what those last few weeks and months had been like. She would picture the lock of hair that seemed to always fall down on his forehead and the way he would raise his eyebrows with such a cute expression. Janelle could see him standing there in the house, before he had got so sick, with that certain way he would always stand. His smile, that everyone loved, had been something all that had known him cherished. He seemed to give everyone strength to keep going with that wonderful smile and his strong will to live. He had a fighting spirit right up to his last breath. He had courage and hope of life hereafter.

II Timothy 4:7-8 *" I have fought a good fight, I have finished my course, I have kept the faith: Henceforth there is laid up for me a crown of righteousness, which the Lord, the righteous judge, shall give me at that day: and not to me only, but unto all them also that love his appearing. "*

Now James is reaping the results of his faith in God and his courage and willingness to not give in to depression, bitterness, or turn his back on God when things got tough.

God's love was so visible in James while he had been here on earth. He had set good examples for others by the way he lived his life. Remembering how strong, brave and loving he had been made her want to be brave now and not be left behind in depression and this forest of grieving forever. With tears flowing from remembering her last time with her beloved James, before he passed away, she knew that in order to keep her promise to him she had to get back to the business of living, and doing God's will while she remained here on earth.

Janelle knew it was time for her to leave the forest of gloom, emptiness, and despair behind. It was time to move forward. She felt she needed to stop focusing on her loss and start thinking about the future. She discovered that moving forward is good, but she had tried to move forward too quickly and wasn't ready. It was too soon. The more she had tried to think of herself and what she wanted in life, the more she thought of James and how much she missed him. Trying to not think about him at all and getting on with her life, she began to realize that she loved him too much to leave him behind. He was still so much a part of her that trying to leave him behind was extremely painful. She just couldn't walk away from her memories. She knew that he wasn't coming back and she was doing the right thing by moving on with her life, but she had gone about it in the wrong way and was trying to move too quickly. Some had warned her she was trying to rush things. They were right, and she found herself once again feeling intense pain from her loss. Trying to move forward so quickly as she had seen others do when they lost their loved ones didn't work for her and had thrown her into a deeper depression of grief and despair.

She became very discouraged and lost courage and hope of ever leaving this dense forest of darkness. The home that she had shared with James and that had brought her so much joy in the past had now become her dark forest. Once again she fought desperately this natural state of depression. Depression, though, can also be a very destructive part of living. She didn't like these feelings of depression and had seen what it had done to so many people. She prayed in desperation that God would help her not to continue to sink deeper into the darkness.

Nahum 1:7 *"The Lord is good, a strong hold in the day of trouble; and he knoweth them that trust in him."*

Janelle kept telling herself that she could do all things through Christ, which strengthened her.

Philippians 4:13 *"I can do all things through Christ which strengthenth me."*

She questioned in her mind how long she must walk in the shadows of the death of the one she loved, feeling such intense pain and loneliness. Would this intense pain ever go away?

Could her shattered heart ever be a whole heart again? Would there always be this emptiness, loneliness, and darkness that completely surrounded her day after day? In her heart she knew the answers can be found in God's word.

Hebrews 4:16 *"Let us therefore come boldly unto the throne of grace,that we may obtain mercy, and find grace to help in time of need."*

John 14:14, 15, 18 *"If ye shall ask any thing in my name, I will do it. If ye love me, keep my commandments. I will not leave you comfortless. I will come to you."*

The death of someone you love can be like driving in the fog on a dark night when your headlights seem to give you little or no light to guide you through the darkness and the fog. You cannot see very far ahead. This leaves you feeling uncertain and uneasy. It can be very frightening being so unsure of what is up ahead in the darkness.

Death has left Janelle feeling as though she was trying to move ever so slowly through this mist, fog, and darkness. If she could keep moving, sooner or later she knew she would find a way to leave the darkness, fog and uncertainty behind. Trying to move forward can be very frightening at times. You strain your eyes to try to see into the darkness and fog. You are afraid to stop because of the dangers that lurk in the fog, yet afraid to move forward. Janelle just wanted desperately to escape the fog, density, and uncertainty of the forest.

Being a child of God, you know God is the light that will lead you out of the fog and the darkness. She knew she must reach out to God to find that way of escape.

Psalms 27:1 *"The Lord is my light and my salvation; whom shall I fear? The Lord is the strength of my life; of whom shall I be afraid?"*

SANDRA JAY KINSLOW

Proverbs 3:5-6 *"Trust in the Lord with all thine heart; and lean not unto thine own understanding. In all thy ways acknowledge him, and he shall direct thy path."*

She longed to find a place of peace, joy, happiness and sunlight. She knew there was laughter in the hearts of many and people who sing with such heartfelt inspiration. It felt like it had been a long time since she had laughed, smiled from within and been extremely happy. The loss of James had left her feeling miserable, cold, lonely and so unhappy.

God is there to help you, but you must be willing to let Him. Just the knowledge that God can save you is not enough to escape the forest. You must be willing to allow your Heavenly Savior to help you. It is hard to cope with some things of this life alone. You need help during the troubling times of your life. Janelle needed God's help.

Psalms 62:7-8 *"In God is my salvation and my glory: the rock of my strength, and my refuge, is in God. Trust in him at all times; ye people, pour out your heart before him: God is a refuge for us. Selah."*

Her loss was an individual loss that affected her one way and yet her children felt the loss of their dad in another way. Everyone has to deal with the death of a loved one in his or her own way. Only God knows just how much an individual is really hurting deep down inside.

Salvation is also an individual thing. No one can acquire salvation for you. Someone can show you through God's words how to reach out to Him and pray with you. They can encourage you to turn your troubles over to Him and let him come into your life. Salvation is free to all who will just ask for it. When you become a child of God, you will never have to taste death. You will experience only the physical death, the shedding of this earthly body. You will live forever with God when you become a child of the King. He made life eternal, possible through the death, burial, and resurrection of His son Jesus. He is our beacon in the fog and our hope for the day, and life eternal in Heaven. He is the lighthouse to give guidance in the storms. He is our light in darkness.

28

Acts 26:18 "To open their eyes, and to turn them from darkness to light, and from the power of Satan unto God; that they may receive forgiveness of sins, and inheritance among them which are sanctified by faith that is in me."

Most people realize that its dangerous to stop on a busy highway on a foggy night. You also don't stop living just because someone dies. When you stop eating, sleeping, and doing the things essential to life, you are essentially stopping on the busy highway of life.

Leaving God out of your life is like driving in the fog without your headlights or walking down a dark road without a flashlight. You stumble, fall and become confused when you can't see where you are going. Drugs, alcohol, death of a loved one, divorce, financial losses can all be factors in your life that create your world of darkness. These are some of the many things that can bring depression and grief into your life. Janelle was experiencing that grief and its depression.

Eating alone was hard. Janelle missed looking up and seeing James across the table from her. It was hard adjusting to cooking for just herself. She didn't have any appetite and had to just make herself prepare a full-course meal. It was much easier to snack but not very healthy. She knew the importance of eating and eating regularly, but she found no enjoyment in eating alone.

In the past she had always had such a true fighting spirit within her that gave her the drive necessary to keep going when things get tough. She had fought a lot of good battles for what she had known to be a battle for what was right and good. She was not a quitter yet found this battle to be the toughest battle of all battles. It is one battle she had been unable to fight alone. She had met her match in this battle of the death of her true love. All her efforts to move forward on her own had proved futile. When she had attempted to do it on her own, she found it had brought even more pain and grief into her life. It had limited her vision of what was up ahead.

She just wanted to find the way to the meadows beyond the forest of darkness. The devil tried to discourage her and make her believe that God wasn't there. He tried to convince her that God had abandoned her and if He loved her so much she wouldn't be hurting, and God wouldn't have taken her beloved James away. The devil loves darkness and if you listen to him, he will discourage you and you will never leave the forest. Janelle knew that through prayer she could fight off the devil.

In her heart she knew that James had suffered enough and that God in His mercy took him out of this world of suffering. The devil would have loved to convince her to believe otherwise, if she had listened to him.

It takes courage to resist the devil and flee from him. This courage to resist the devil can be found in trusting God and relying on Him. If you want to leave your troubles behind, you have to get up and move away from the darkness. When you return to God, He can restore peace within.

John 16:33 *"These things I have spoken unto you, that in me ye might have peace. In the world ye shall have tribulation: but be of good cheer; I have overcome the world."*

James had fought the fight; he kept the faith and henceforth, there was laid up for him a crown of righteousness. She knew if she was going to join James one day as she had promised him prior to his death, then she must do the work of the Lord. By her actions she would be able to show others that God was living within her and that her hope and courage had come from God. For her, survival came from faith in God, belief in Him and His ability to guide and help her.

I Thessalonians 1:3 *"Remembering without ceasing your work of faith, and labor of love and patience of hope in our Lord Jesus Christ, in the sight of God and our Father:"*

II Timothy 4:5 *"But watch thou in all things, endure afflictions, do the work of an evangelist, make full proof of thy ministry."*

Revelations 22:12 *"And, behold, I come quickly; and my reward is with me, to give every man according as his work shall be."*

She realized and admitted after James' death she was mentally and physically exhausted, and to some extent her faith had been tested. God had always been there for her all that time. He had his hand reaching out to steady her, brace her or lift her up if she fell. He had given her wisdom through the knowledge of the words of God. This had helped her face difficult things in life. She was learning that the death of a loved one could destroy you if you let it.

Doctors today are able to do miraculous things. They can prolong life with the use of certain medication, machines and other devices. Their abilities to save lives are limited, but God is the one that gives life and is the one that in the end makes the final decisions as to when that life will end. How you live your life here on earth will determine where you go after you leave this earth. Doctors can help you physically. God is the one that you must turn to for spiritual healing. He is the greatest physician of all. We will all have to stand before God when our life is finished here and will be held accountable for our deeds done on earth. Her desire was to be a faithful servant of God to the end.

Psalms 121:1-2 *"I will lift up mine eyes unto the hills, from whence cometh my help. My help cometh from the Lord, which made heaven and earth."*

Chapter 2
Lonely Nights And Dark Days

The darkness of her forest was darkest at night. Janelle found herself waking up to check on her husband only to realize he was not there anymore. He was in Heaven. It was hard to go back to sleep after waking up and realizing that you were alone and he was not there anymore. She found it was easier to work until she was so tired at night that she fell asleep from exhaustion. Most of the nights following James' death she would cry herself to sleep. Other nights she would awake many times during the night as she had done so often in the past to check on him. She had become accustomed to sleeping very lightly at nights, so she could hear him if he had seizures during the night. Even the slightest squeak of his bed would awaken her immediately. Prayers seemed to help when she was lying in bed unable to sleep. Praying eases the pain and eventually she would drift back to sleep. Trying to determine which bed to sleep in at night was a problem for her. Not having James by her side made her night lonely, and she tried switching from one bedroom to the other one in hopes that in doing so it would be possible to get some rest.

Putting the daybed and hospital bed up in their family room had proved to be a good solution for taking care of James when he became bedfast and needed lots of care. Janelle being in the same room with him at night had made him feel more secure. It had been easy for her to watch him closely when he was in the family room and not down in a bedroom shut off from the rest of the house. James had been able to see her easily when she was in the kitchen or utility room, where she had an office. The family room had become their whole world.

His brother put up a wheelchair ramp due to the family room being a sunken family room, prior to James becoming totally bedfast. By having the ramp you could get him in his wheelchair, and take him up into the main part of the house.

He had a television, radio, stereo, magazines and books to enjoy. The last year of his life he slept a great deal and lost interest in television and other things.

After he passed away, Janelle had all the medical equipment and ramp removed and the room became a family room again. At first she found it easier to sleep in the family room rather than the bedrooms. She felt close to him in that room. She could still envision him lying in his bed and waving with his fingers as she walked past. He would always smile at her and nod his head when she would check on him as she did so often during the nights and days prior to his death

When she was having trouble sleeping she could remember so many events of the past, like this one particular day when she had gone out to check on him. He had become unable to communicate verbally.

On this particular day he looked sad and didn't have his usual smile. She gave him a big hug and told him how much she loved him and how special he was to her. She had reassured him that it was a joy to be the one taking care of him because she loved him so much. Nothing seemed to cheer him that day. After hugging him she told him she missed his being able to hug her. He nodded sadly. James had not only lost his ability to communicate but had also become so weak that he didn't have the strength to roll over or even raise his arms up off of the bed. Tears had come to her eyes as she thought how sad it was that he was no longer able to wrap his arms around her and hug and hold her in his arms. She had laid the upper part of her body across his chest as she stood by his bed and then picked up each one of his arms and draped them over her shoulders. Janelle could feel the weight of his arms on her shoulder and back. Glancing up at him she had seen tears in his eyes and a big smile on his face and he was nodding yes. He had missed being able to hug her too. It was a very special moment for both of them and one she would never forget. As she lay there in the dark, remembering all of this, she could still envision the tears in his eye, and the smile on his face.

James had always found a way to show his love. In spite of his multiple health problems, he was able to communicate his love. Sometimes it would be an expression on his face or the twinkle in his

LOST IN A DARK FOREST

eyes. He would hold her hand and squeeze it gently to assure her of his feelings. On special occasions he would ask their daughter to go shopping for him so she could purchase something he had wanted to give to his wife, the woman he loved. He relied on her to take care of those personal needs and relied on their son to help with taking care of the car. He was a Certified Master Technician and his dad was very proud of him and his accomplishments and knew he would be able to take care of any mechanical needs she had. Not being able to talk to his family he had learned how to express his love to each one of them in different ways. He loved his kids, grandkids, family and friends with a very special love.

They had faced the difficulties of life together side by side, hand in hand. Their love had strengthened with each and every day of their marriage. Just as they had faced life together hand in hand, side-by-side, they had faced death together holding hands when God called James home to Heaven. It had been her prayer that if it be God's will, He would permit her to be by James' side, holding his hand when the angel of death came to carry James home to be with God. God granted her wish and Janelle was there telling him how much she loved him, holding his hand, and reassuring him she loved him and of the love of his family and friends.

As is the case in most deaths, your mind goes back to the day of the funeral. It had been a hard day for everyone that loved James so much. She remembered in particular walking up to the casket after he had done a beautiful job of paying tribute to James in the message he had delivered. Her daughter and husband had been standing on one side of her and her son and his wife had been on the other side of her. They had been supporting her with their love and strength. As she had stood by James' casket, she felt the most excruciating, crushing pain. The pain was beyond anything that words could describe. Janelle had never experienced this much pain in her life. She found it difficult to breathe or even swallow. She recalled looking up into the face of her dad that she loved and respected so much and said to him, 'It hurts so bad.' He had hugged her and nodded yes. He understood some of the pain she felt as he had cared for her mother for many years. It had been 14 years since her death, but he still remembered the pain that he felt when her mother had passed away. Dad had been very fortunate later after her

35

death to meet some one very special that he had fallen in love with and married. She had become a very special mom to Janelle. On that day, though, he could understand her pain as he hugged his daughter.

Janelle had dreamed several years prior to James' death that he had died, and she had awoken in tears, and had checked to make sure James was alive and okay. On the day of James' funeral she remembered the pain being so bad in that dream that she had about James dying, but as she stood there by his casket and looked at James for the last time she knew the pain she was feeling was even worse than the dream. It was an unbearable pain that she still felt at times even today.

God had been her refuge and strength on the day when they buried James. She could not have made it that day without His help. Janelle knew that she could not have made it through all the time of sleepless nights and long days of caring for him when he was so sick had it not been for the strength that God had given her. From the moment she had accepted Christ as her Lord and Savior, He had become her refuge, strength and comforter. He was her guide throughout life. She knew from the scriptures she could count on Him anytime day or night.

Psalms 38:39 *"But the salvation of the righteous is of the Lord: he is their strength in the time of trouble."*

Matthew 28:20 *"Teaching them to observe all things whatsoever I have commanded you: and, lo, I am with you always, even unto the end of the world. Amen"*

God would be by her side right to the very end of life. She had seen the peace and assurance in James' life because James had known that when he left this earth he would be spending an eternity in Heaven with God.

John 14:27 *"Peace I leave with you, my peace I give unto you: not as the world giveth, give I unto you. Let not your heart be troubled, neither let it be afraid."*

Jesus when He knew He must face death and took upon Himself all the sins of the world by crucifixion faced His darkest time here on earth. He had gone into the Garden of Gethsemane to pray to His Father, "not

LOST IN A DARK FOREST

my will but thine be done." Jesus' death on the cross made it possible for us to have the assurance of a home in heaven if we will become a child of our Heavenly Father and worship Him all the days of our lives. The death, burial, and resurrection have given us hope of life eternal. Because of this hope Janelle knew that she would see James again.

Janelle knew she would never forget a young couple in James' family who were among the many that had come to the hospital often and especially that last week that James lived. This couple was James' nephew, wife and daughter. They had given them hugs and cried with them and shared many things that had been painful for them to share. They had felt in sharing these things it would be helpful in understanding the final stages prior to James' death. Not only was she a nurse and could explain things in medical terms, but also had known firsthand what they were going through. They had sat by the bedside of their son, who was only seven year old, when he had been in critical condition in Children's Hospital. They had experienced some of the things that James had been going through because of their son. Now James was up in Heaven with their son and other loved ones. Those moments spent with them in the hospital would always be cherished because of the way they had reached out with such love. They had shared the last painful moments about their son with them in spite of the pain it had caused them remembering all that had happened to their son. It had helped them during those last moments with James. Indeed, what beautiful love dwells in the hearts of those who truly know God? These were Christians who had learned how to lean on God and draw strength from Him.

God came to Janelle in the darkness, deep within her forest in a most unusual way. After James' death, her forest had become even more dismal when she learned that her total income each month would only be $176. She had been shocked when she realized due to contract changes in the company from which her husband had retired on disability, this would be all she was entitled to receive. She knew she could never make it on such a small income. After so many years of caring for James she was totally exhausted. She was in no shape to even find a job, much less being able to work each day.

After getting this bleak news over the phone, Janelle had walked out to her little garden, a favorite spot in the yard, and had lain down in a hammock hanging between two shade trees. She cried and prayed to God, *"Lord, how can I possibly live on so little at this time when I am unable to work?"* She knew the meager little savings she had would not last long and some of that would be needed to pay off some of the medical bills. She had felt such a burden and so discouraged.

God had given her an answer right away. After lying there for some time crying and praying, she had opened my eyes and sitting on the limb just above her were two of the healthiest birds you have ever seen. There was a cardinal and blue jay sitting side by side. You don't see these two birds sitting on the same limb very often. God had sent these two beautiful, fat, healthy birds as a reminder to Janelle, if He cares for the fowls of the air, how much more He cares for his children. Janelle wiped the tears from her eyes and knew from that moment on that with God's help she would be okay. She closed her eyes and said a prayer of thanks to God for His answer.

Matthew 6:25-34 *"Therefore I say unto you, Take no thought for your life, what ye shall eat, or what ye shall drink; nor yet for your body, what ye shall put on. Is not the life more than meat, and the body than raiment? Behold the fowls of the air: for they sow not, neither do they reap, nor gather into barns; yet your heavenly Father feedeth them. Are ye not much better than they? And why take ye thought for raiment? Consider the lilies of the field, how they grow; they toil not, neither do they spin: And yet I say unto you That Solomon in all his glory was not arrayed like one of these. Wherefore, if God so clothes the grass of the field, which today is and tomorrow is cast into the oven, shall he not much more clothe you, O ye of little faith? Therefore take no thought saying, What shall we eat? Or What shall we drink? Or Wherewithal shall we be clothed? (For after all these things do the Gentiles seek:) for your heavenly Father knoweth that ye have need of all of these things. But seek ye first the kingdom of God, and his righteousness; and all these things shall be added unto you. Take therefore no thought or the morrow: for the morrow shall take thought for the things of itself. Sufficient unto the day is the evil thereof"*

She began to see God's promises fulfilled since the death of her beloved James. There had been such an outpouring of gifts. Checks had come from people she never dreamed would send money to help out. The food and other gifts that were given had been so much help. There had been over 200 phone calls in the first three months after his death with messages of encouragement and love. Many had sent cards and mailed messages over the computer with words of comfort. God had been meeting her needs in such special ways. He had heard her cries and knew what her needs were.

God can see in the darkness and He knows what you are in need of even before you ask. Some have questioned why pray at all if He already knows what you need. Prayer is opening your heart up to God and allowing the Holy Spirit to speak on your behalf. It opens up communications to God and the scriptures say we often have not because we ask not.

Philippians 4:6 *"Be careful for nothing: but in every thing by prayer and supplication with thanksgiving let your requests be made know unto God."*

Philippians 4:19 *"But my God shall supply all your need according to his riches in glory by Christ Jesus."*

Matthew 21:22 *"And all things, whatsoever ye shall ask in prayer, believing, ye shall receive."*

God loves you and cares for you. Janelle knew in her heart that she could leave this morbid place behind because with God there was hope.

Psalms 121:1-8 *"I will lift up mine eyes unto the hills, from whence cometh my help. My help cometh from the Lord, which made heaven and earth. He will not suffer thy foot to be moved: he that keepeth thee will not slumber. Behold, he that keepeth Israel shall neither slumber nor sleep. The Lord is thy keeper: the Lord is thy shade upon thy right hand. The sun shall not smite thee by day, nor the moon by night. The Lord shall preserve thee from all evil: he shall preserve thy soul. The Lord shall preserve thy going out and thy coming in from this time forth, and even for evermore."*

God carried Janelle when she became too tired to walk. He had protected her and had been her shield and armor against the devil and those that would have harmed her.

Psalms 27:1 *"The Lord is my light and my salvation; whom shall I fear? The Lord is the strength of my life; of whom shall I be afraid,"* God is truly the Great I Am.

Janelle can slowly feel her strength returning. She is grateful for the love and care that she had received from family and friends. Thanks to that care she was not forced to have to find work immediately. Several future job opportunities had opened up for her, which had allowed time to heal and regain her physical strength. Time had also helped her to become more stable emotionally and physically. Her church had also been so supportive, loving and caring. It was a small country church, but so much love could be felt there.

Janelle could feel God slowly leading her into the future. He knew Janelle needed to go slow due to the fatigue and loss she had suffered. God had cared for her much like an earthly mother or father cares for their child.

The greatest physician of all is God Himself. His hand of healing was upon her. Just as some wounds are deep and require more time for healing, a broken heart also takes time to mend. She could feel the touch of the Master's hand as she reached often blindly into the gloomy and morbid forest. She held fast to His outstretched hand as He led her through the paths of complete blackness. God would bring Janelle back into the warmth of His light and love and guide her safely through the dangers that are there within the density of the forest.

Psalms 119:105 *"Thy word is a lamp unto my feet, and a light unto my path."*

The winter had been long, cold and lonely. The trees around her had shut out the warmth of what little sunshine had been visible during the winter months. She eagerly waited for the chance to enjoy once again spring and summer. Janelle longed or the time when she could leave this drab, dismal place of obscurity. She knew there were blessings and sunshine in the meadows beyond the trees. The sunlight would warm her cold body and brighten the days. Spring would bring new hope. The trees in the meadows would bud out and produce beautiful leaves. The flowers with their blossoms would give out sweet fragrances and their blossoms a thing of beauty. The dried grass from winter would come to life during spring and become a carpet of greenery. The beautiful birds returning from their winter habitats could be heard singing their melodious songs. God's beauty could be found in the meadows beyond this bleak and dreary forest.

There are many things that bring healing and God's beauty that surrounds us is one of those methods of healing. Walking helps to bring about healing and strengthening of the mind and body. Praying and trusting in God renews spiritual strength and you grow stronger in the Lord.

I Thessalonians 5:17 *"Pray without ceasing."*

Sometimes healing can be found in your own yard. A neighbor had helped to construct a goldfish pond for James to enjoy shortly before he passed away. Sidewalks had been made so his wheelchair could be used outside on the sidewalk, where the pond was. Unfortunately by the time the pond had been completed James had made a turn for the worse and only got to enjoy the pond briefly.

The goldfish pond was surrounded by flowers, rocks, and other greenery. Inside the gold fishpond had been a fountain in the center and a little waterfall in the back where water trickles down some rocks. The sounds of the water spraying and dripping off rocks can be very soothing, relaxing and enjoyable. This had become a place of healing for her now that she was nearing the edge of the forest. The depth of the forest had kept her from hearing the sounds of the water, or the birds singing, but now she could hear the sounds the water makes when it is trickling off the waterfall. In her mind she could envision the flowers and fish swimming below the water. She could have never enjoyed the sounds of the birds or the water falling from the rocks deep within that blackened forest if she had chosen to stay within the forest. Janelle is so glad she is no longer deaf to sounds around her. Unfortunately many don't know God and these people often turn to things of this world when they are struggling in their own dark forest. The devil loves it when you are feeling down and out and depressed. It delights him to see you wallow in self-pity and hide in the darkness that surrounds you. He will bring you temptations even into the darkness to continue to tempt you. He will make sure you never want to see the light of day. Satan knows what your weaknesses are and uses any means necessary to supply you with those things you reach for in desperation. Some will turn to God for help and flee the devil and his temptations. Others will turn to drugs, alcohol, suicide, total denial, or just become absorbed in things of this world. Many search for a quick fix to solve their problems. The devil knows exactly what to do to entice you with a quick fix to your problems. He will do everything in his power to destroy you. The devil doesn't care about your soul or what happens to you.

There are many things that create forests of darkness in our lives. Whether you are a Christian or not, each and everyone will have to face difficult times in their lives. None will be spared death. We will either lose a loved one or be facing our own physical death. In the end God holds our lives in His hands. If you are a Christian you will know death only in the physical sense when you shed your earthly body. If you are a sinner, and have not been saved by the grace of God, you will stand before God to be held accountable for your sins and face an eternity in Hell.

While Janelle was in the deep depths of the forest, she was saddened to hear the cries of those who were lost in their world of drugs and alcohol. For some of those who are lost to drugs and other addictions, she can only hope they get help before it is too late. Is there hope at all for those lost in this deep part of the forest? Yes, there is hope for them. There is a way out of the forest of addiction and abuse.

Chapter 3
Children and Adults
Lost In The Forest of Darkness
From Drugs, Alcohol, and Sexual Abuse

Janelle noticed that within her darkened forest, there were some young adults that were lost in a forest that was perhaps even darker than the one she had been experiencing. You could hear their screams and cries out for help all during the day and night. Many of the problems they were dealing with were things that some of them were not even responsible for. They were things that they had no control of. Some of these problems were the results of their parents' divorce, or the loss of a parent due to death. There were many different kinds of things that had brought these young children and young adults into this forest that Janelle longed to be free from.

Children today are being exposed to an adult world that is filled with sin often at a very early age. They are exposed to things they do not know how to deal with, because they are often not mature enough to know how to handle certain situations. Many, fearing they will look stupid or dumb, will just simply mimic or do what they see other doing. They might not even want to do what they are doing, but don't know what else to do. If it is something that is wrong they often feel afraid to stop for fear of being tormented by their peers. The ones they mimic often look confident and mature so they will continue to follow their examples. They want to appear mature even though they are definitely not mature enough for what they are being exposed to. Following the example of others who are not mature in Christ can cause them to travel down a road of sin and destruction. To keep from looking like a little kid they will continue to do what they are doing in order to look

SANDRA JAY KINSLOW

mature. Many of these young kids are not mature enough for the things they are being a part of and they go spiraling into a deep depression.

Drug abuse, drinking, prostitution, stealing, lying, cheating are just some of the many temptations that young people are up against each and every day. When they get caught up in some of these activities, they begin to live with guilt, and their self-esteem can be damaged. If they are not given counseling, preferably Christian counseling, with the word of God, and shown how God does truly love them and cares about them, they can sink deep and deeper into this darkness and sin.

Some people through bad choices in life will end up in this forest of blackness, from drug abuse or alcoholic abuse. They want to be cool and do what everyone else is doing by taking drugs or drinking with the group. Many of these become addicted to the drugs or the alcohol. The more they abuse the drugs and drink to excess the darker their world becomes. Ugly trees seem to surround them as they sink deeper in the gloom and desperation that the drugs have brought into their lives.

A life that had once held promise for them now seems hopeless. They wake each morning in search of a new high, a few more drinks, or something to stop the craving, the shakiness and the intense desire for the drugs, or a shot of heroine or something that will calm them down or send them on yet another high. The dangers that these drugs present of death or causing them to do something they wouldn't have done had they not been under the influence of these drugs doesn't seem to matter to them when they are craving these drugs or under its influence. They live from one high to the next from the effects of the drugs or alcohol. Their lives are often filled with nightmares and they fight off the demons of their dense forest. Some resort to suicide to try to escape from the darkness of their addictions. Many are unsuccessful in their attempts to end their lives and their world looks bleaker than before. Attempts to help them leave this ugly abuse behind are often futile because the person does not have the courage or desire to leave it all behind. They are unwilling to fight the demons of drug or alcohol. Unlike James, who had met the monster of death head on, holding tight to the hand of God, many of these people don't even know God. They have never been witnessed to nor have they heard the words of God read to them. They feel all alone and unsure as to how to leave this maze of trees that surround them.

Janelle thinks about all of them as she continues to look for the path that will help her move forward to the sunlight of healing and recovery. She sees how difficult it is for her as she deals daily with her loss and wishes that all of these people that are in so much pain could know the God she knows like she does, so that they wouldn't lose hope and stop trying. She wishes they knew Him personally so that they could with His help overcome these addictions and find true peace. She has so much empathy for them. God loves them just like He loves her, and He doesn't want them to be lost forever. God knows how difficult it is to live right in this sin-filled world and to make the right choices in life is not always easy. God wants to help but if they are unwilling to let Him help them they will never receive the kind of help they need the most.

Janelle knows that whether it's a forest of drugs, alcohol or dealing with the pain and anguish of losing a loved one, you need help. God is the only one that can help. She has seen personally what the abuse of drugs or alcohol can do to people. She has seen the kind of problems it has created in the lives of some she knew personally and was so close to.

Janelle had received news from a family she was very close to regarding their son. He had been having problems with drinking and was found lying dead in a parking lot from alcohol poisoning, only two weeks after he had lost his dad. Here was a young person whose life had been cut short because he was lost in the forest of drinking and possible feelings of regret and remorse. A mother had lost her husband and then two weeks later had lost her son. Her grandchildren had lost their dad.

Is there a way out? Is their hope for those who cannot find their way out? Will she ever recover from her loneliness and her loss? Janelle knows she has God in her heart, and that He is her way out of this horrible forest of pain, loneliness, and obscurity. What about those who don't know God? Will anyone ever be able to reach his or her sad and troubled hearts?

Psalms 25:4,5 *"Shew me thy ways, O Lord; teach me thy paths. Lead me in thy truth, and teach me: for thou art the God of my salvation; on thee do I wait all the day."*

Janelle seeks God and His truths, so that He can lead her in the pathways of salvation, peace and healing. She knows that sometimes the truths are painful and difficult to deal with. You can't live in denial all your life, and sooner or later you are usually forced to deal with the reality of life and its truths.

For the addict it's the realization that they no longer control their lives, that the addiction controls them. They can have no hope of recovery or leaving the forest of abuse until they are willing to face the truth and take control of their lives again.

Sometimes the truth means forcing yourself to come to terms with what pushed you into the forest in the first place. For some it might have been abuse as a child, or peer pressure. Some end up on drugs or drink too much because they were just curious at the start and wanted to know what it was like to get high or get drunk. Many are just weak and can't seem to say NO to the things that they know in their hearts are just not right, yet lack the strength to stand up and simply say NO.

Help is available to everyone. Nothing is more frightening than realizing you are lost. Whether you are lost spiritually or just lost in the forest, help is available. God will send help to you if you will just trust and believe in Him.

Janelle remembered one day her husband having seizures. They were called psychomotor seizures. They were the kind that when the seizure hits you, you just take off in a fast run or walk real fast and are unaware of what you are doing at the time. He had disappeared right out of the yard. People help to search for him with teams of over 500 volunteers, airplanes, people on horseback, and 4-wheelers. Many just lined up in rolls and walked the fields. He had walked off earlier that morning. The search had gone on all day with not even a single footstep visible in the dirt road to help them know which way he might have headed. Janelle was afraid that when he was found it might be too late because one of the aneurisms in the brain was swollen and needed repaired surgically. They had just returned from seeing the neurosurgeon that week. James had taken his guitar outside and was playing it on the front steps when he just disappeared. She had gone to check on him to make sure he was okay when the music had stopped and he was not on the porch. She searched everywhere, and no James. She called neighbors and friends in to help her search and there was not

LOST IN A DARK FOREST

a trace of him. Other volunteers came when they heard and the search continued all day. She felt so helpless while she waited. The fears grew as the evening approached and he had still not been found. She worried that he might have caught a ride with someone in his state of confusion from the seizures. It was a day of walking, searching and pacing floors in hopes they would find him before it was too late.

When James had realized what had happened to him, the day he had wandered off with a seizure, he knew that he was in a forest somewhere. He didn't know how he got there or where all he had been. He just knew he was lost. He called on God to help him. A big dog showed up in the forest out of nowhere. James loved dogs and was very good with animals. He had patted the dog on the head and the dog would bark and start to leave and then come back to him. James knew this dog acted like he wanted him to follow him. The dog looked familiar to him, so he followed the dog and it led him back to the road, where a deputy was patrolling the highway in hopes of finding James. The dog ran out into the road in front of the patrol car, forcing the car to stop, and there was James standing in the fence roll along the edge of the highway. It was dark at that time, and had the animal not run out in front of the patrol car, the deputy probably would have never seen James standing near the bushes near the highway. God sent James help in his forest, by possibly sending this big dog to help him out of the deep part of the forest and back to where he could get help. James was tired and still having seizures but he was alive. It had been a very frightening experience for both of them. Tears could be seen in the eyes of even big grown men when the call came over the police radio that James had been found and was alive. James had his second brain operation only a week after that happened. God had been with him through all of that. James was lost but God knew where he was at and the condition his mind was in and took care of him. James was a child of God and God's hand of protection was there for him.

God was there for Janelle and He can be there for you too. He will not force Himself on you, but just as He had been there for Janelle, waiting for her to trust Him and let Him lead her out of the forest, she knows He will be there for the others who are lost in the forest.

Chapter 4
Job's Darkest Hours

Janelle recalls the story as told in the Bible in the book of Job. This is a story of a faithful and righteous man whose name was Job. This man was wealthy, healthy and a very happy man. He was extremely blessed. He had a good family and ten kids. He loved his wife and she was a good wife. He was loyal and faithful to God.

The devil was upset that Job was so righteous and that God thought so much of Job. He figured if he had a chance to tempt Job and work on him a little bit that God would see that Job was like any other man and would turn his back on God and curse Him.

God allowed the devil to tempt Job because He knew His servant was a good man and that he was faithful to Him. God had faith in Job. The devil just knew that he could succeed in his plans to break Job down and cause him to curse God.

All of Job's neighbors thought highly of him. He was good to everyone and set good examples of righteous living. He was so happy and had such a good life until one day, everything started falling apart.

First he lost his cattle and other valuable herds. They had either been driven off or killed.

He hated to lose such valuable herds but he had his family and his own good health.

The next big blow to Job was the hardest blow of all in my opinion. Job had ten children, that he loved dearly, and his oldest son, who was married, invited all his brothers and sisters to his house for a big party. While everyone was at the party, a huge storm came up and blew the house down, killing everyone inside. One person, who escaped the wrath of the storm ran to tell Job all that had happened. Janelle found it hard to imagine the grief and torture of losing ten children all at the same time. How very devastating that had to have been for Job and his wife. For a family to lose even one child much less every one of their children at one time would be hard for anyone.

Job was filled with so much sorrow that he did what was a custom in old Bible times when someone was sad. He shaved his head and tore his clothing—or, as the Bible says, rent his clothes. He couldn't understand why so much was happening and felt such pain from all he had lost. Instead of cursing God, though, he called out to God and said, 'The Lord gave, and the Lord hath taken away; blessed be the name of the Lord.'

The old devil just knew that this would be all it took to make Job curse God. The devil could hardly believe it. He had been so sure that Job would turn against God when he was ruined financially. When that didn't change the way Job felt about God, the devil was sure that the loss of all of his children would cause him to have doubts and cause him to lose faith. The devil approached God again and asked for one more chance to prove that he could make Job turn away from God. He figured that if Job was afflicted with sores all over his body and was in such agony and physical pain that would be all it would take for him to curse God. He figured a man would give almost anything to save himself.

It was hard to picture someone able to tolerate boils all over their body. Job was in such misery that he went out under a tree and sat in ashes. He would take a piece of pottery to scrap the pus off the boils. From what little Janelle knew about boils they are very painful, and Job was covered in boils.

Job's wife was not as strong spiritually. She wasn't afflicted with boils but having lost all of their children, wealth, and then seeing her husband covered in boils caused her to beg Job to curse God and die. Job told her she was a foolish woman and that God had been there for them during the best of times and He would be there for them during the worst of times. She was unable to see it like Job and had a difficult time accepting all that happened. She was in her own dark forest of despair.

Job was well liked in his community and especially by his neighbors. They knew about all of his problems and felt they should go and comfort him and talk with him. The neighbors found him sitting in the field covered with ashes. He was scraping the pus off the boils. They were deeply concerned about their friend.

They all sat down with him and the first neighbor spoke. He suggested to Job that perhaps Job had sinned against God and had made God angry. He was sure that this had to be the reason that Job lost everything he had. He could not imagine any other reason a man would lose everything.

Job replied to his first friend that he was surprised that his neighbor and friend would say such a thing, knowing that he was a righteous man, and didn't believe God would bring punishment upon him for something he hadn't done. Job knew he had been faithful to God. He could not believe God would send this kind of punishment for being faithful.

The second neighbor thought that maybe instead of Job sinning, it must have been one of his children who had sinned and displeased God.

The third neighbor agreed with the first. He, too, was convinced that Job must have done something bad. He was sure that Job had sinned and God was angry.

Job was upset with his neighbors, who were also his friends. He felt they should have known better. They had seen his plight as a curse brought upon Job from having angered God. They did not see it as a test of Job's faith and loyalty to God. 'Though he slay me yet will I trust in God,' Job told his friends.

He felt that even if his skin rotted away and he died, he would see God. He told them he felt his faith was being tested with all the losses and affliction and that he would be okay, because he loved God. He refused to turn his back on God.

While they were all sitting in the field and had finished talking to Job, God appeared to all of them out of a whirlwind. He spoke to Job and his friends. When God had finished talking to them Job realized that even in his efforts to be so righteous in reality we are all sinners in the eyes of the one who created the very heavens and earth. Job cried out to God in humbleness and asked for His forgiveness.

Even though Job had not knowingly sinned against God, all that had happened to him humbled him. God had mercy upon him.

God had given the neighbors instructions what he wanted them to do. He was not pleased with the attitudes of Job's friends. Job needed them and their support. God told them to bring Job seven bullocks and seven rams and offer up a burnt offering. He told Job to pray for each of the neighbors.

During Biblical times, animals were used as a sacrifice for the forgiveness of sins. When Jesus was crucified, he took upon himself the sins of man and the sacrifice of animals was no longer necessary. Jesus had become the supreme sacrifice for the sins of mankind.

Job did what God had instructed him to do and sacrificed the animals and prayed for his friends. Things began to change for Job. When you are going through a bad time in your life and you pray and reach out to others, healing will begin. Job prayed for his friends and he saw the healing take place.

After the boils healed and Job regained his strength, his neighbors came to him with gifts and things to help him get another start in life. God was pleased to see the response but God was still taking care of Job. He blessed him with twice as much as he had before and even blessed him with ten more children. God rewarded Job for his righteousness and his faith. Faithfulness to God may not result in great wealth on this earth but He has promised us blessings and rewards beyond our imagination in the hereafter. It is hard for us to even begin to imagine the beauty of Heaven and rewards for our faithfulness.

When Janelle thought about Job in this story told in the Bible, and all he had endured and yet remained faithful to God, she was strengthened by his faith in God. He did indeed set good examples not only for his neighbors and friends, but also for us today.

Job turned to God for help and did not blame God or become bitter when his whole world fell apart. Many people blame God for all the bad things that happen in their lives. Job didn't understand all the things that happened. He just knew he served a God that loved him and had been there for him during the good times and would be there for him during the bad times. In his darkest hours and in the darkest part of his forest, Job still reached out to God and never lost faith. Job returned to the meadows and left the forest because he trusted and believed in God.

Job's friends misjudged him when he was suffering so much. Sometimes your friends will say things to you that will upset you as

LOST IN A DARK FOREST

well. They don't mean any harm, but things will be said that will be difficult for you to accept or understand. These people usually mean well but are at a loss as to how to help. God knows what you are really thinking and understands even when others might misjudge you like Jobs friends misjudged him. Be grateful for your friends and their attempts to try and help. It is a blessing to have family and friends by your side during the troubling times of life. Just being able hear the words "I am so sorry and I care" can mean so much to someone who is grieving. Having friends close by had helped Janelle to heal and had given her encouragement during the darkest times. God had brought very special people into her life, and because of Job's faithlness God had rewarded him, and even though she didn't know what was up ahead, she knew if she could hold on to her faith and keep her eyes focused on God that she would make it.

Healing comes from turning things over to God. For Janelle it had come slowly. It is unfair to the person who might be grieving to tell that individual that they haven't grieved long enough or they are grieving too long. No person will necessarily react to his or her grief in the same way nor will they heal in the same amount of time. God knows you on the inside and people see you on the outside. Some had told her she was grieving too long and others said she hadn't grieved long enough. There had been times when she would have a smile on her face and yet inside her heart was bursting with pain. Even when her precious James was alive, there were times when things were really difficult and yet she would be smiling and trying her best to keep her spirits up when inside she was filled with deep concern. People looking at her on the outside would think she was doing great, not realizing that on the inside she was praying continuously for more strength and courage. God knew the pain she was in from watching her loved one in such bad health for so many years. He knew how much she loved him and the deep concern she had felt continuously for him. God could see into her troubled soul now and was giving her the strength needed to keep going. He had also seen her grief and was there for her now, just as He had been there for Job. She wasn't sure how long she would grieve the loss of her husband or if she would ever completely get over losing him, but she knew that God would be there for her always.

She had thought of Job so often during the past 30 years of her life.

SANDRA JAY KINSLOW

When she thought things in life couldn't get any worse, they did. As Janelle sat sadly recalling the things that Job had gone through she could also relate to Job's wife and the pain she must have felt. Knowing the pain she felt at this time from losing her companion, she could only imagine the pain that Job's wife and her husband felt after losing everything they had and all of their children at one time. Like Job, she could not always understand why things happen like they do. It rains on the just and the unjust but when God is a part of your life you have Someone to turn to for help. Job found blessings that he could have never imagined because of his faithfulness to God. He never turned his back on God or cursed Him as his wife had told him to do and he never lost sight of God even in his darkest hours. Job's forest was dark and lonely, but God was always there, and the angels of God were there to minister to his needs. Janelle knows that just as God was there for Job, He was there for her too, meeting her needs, and that if she is faithful and keeps her eyes focused on God, she will receive blessings from just the fellowship with her Heavenly Father. Right now she knew she must focus on finding her way back to a life of sunlight, joy and happiness, that doesn't exist in this deep dark forest of death.

Chapter 5
From Darkness to Light

God was there for Janelle day after day. He brought many wonderful friends into her life during her time of grieving and healing. It took courage for Janelle to reach out and try new and different things. God seemed to be closing doors and opening other doors, but Janelle knew she had to have the courage to move on with her life before God could reveal what He had in store for her.

The edge of the forest was in sight and Janelle was excited. She had been longing for this light at the end of the forest and she could see it off in the distance. She had come so far and had been through so much pain, but God had never once left her side. There were events and things that happened that amazed her. She marveled at how God always seemed to send the right people into her life at the right time.

Shortly after James' death, she had got a phone call from a friend she had known since childhood. She had invited Janelle to go with her and spend time with some of the other members of her family. Janelle had not seen some of them since she was a girl. Janelle was reluctant to go because she felt she was not good company, but with some encouragement from her friend and her own family, she decided to accept the invitation. She had known this beautiful family since she was a young girl and her father had been their pastor. Their home was her favorite place to go after church each Sunday. It was a beautiful Christian family, and a very close family. Their mom had been such an inspiration to Janelle when she was a girl. To her that mother was one of the sweetest mothers she had ever known. She was looking forward to seeing her again. It had been a long time since Janelle had seen their mother. Janelle had kept in touch with some of the family over the years. She had lived near Carla when she and James had lived up north.

Janelle had a great visit with Carla and her whole family. The family was so kind to her and so caring and the time spent with them was good. God had sent this beautiful family back into Janelle's life. She was blessed and touched by their kindness and concerns for her. It was great being back in touch with the whole family. They shared many visits together after that first visit shortly after James' death. God was meeting many of her needs through this loving and caring family. It was great having their love and friendship. Each one of the family seemed to bring something special into Janelle's life. They were easy to talk to, a lot of fun, and a joy to be with.

After a period of time had gone by, God sent yet more blessings. Twin brothers had relocated to the town where Janelle lived. She had known one of the twins' wife when she had been a little girl so it was nice having them there close. They had a little boy that she adored and he would call her Grandma, because his grandma lived a long ways off and Janelle loved him just like he was one of her own grandkids. God knew Janelle had a special love for children and they seemed to touch her in ways no one else could.

The twin brothers were very gifted and one was a youth minister. The other one was music director in church. Together they had written this beautiful musical, called *Jobsong*. Both of them encouraged her to audition for a part in that musical that would be shown in the theater there in the town where she lived. Janelle at first was reluctant, since she hadn't done much singing in years. She loved music, and with their encouragement, she did audition and got a part in the musical. She mostly sang in the chorus, but that was enough. She was still grieving her loss of James, and didn't want any part that she had to memorize. She was still having problems remembering things and didn't want the responsibility of learning so much. She wasn't sure if she was even able to do the musical, much less have a part in it. During the rehearsals God brought new people into her life. Each one of the members of this cast seemed to realize her need to be loved and gave her so many hugs and encouragement and understanding. They all seemed eager to help her and make her feel a part of what was going on. It took courage to reach out and try this at this time in her life. Janelle wasn't sure if she could do this, so soon after James' death, but felt this was God's will. The blessings were many and the joys of knowing you were telling the story of Job on stage was something very special for Janelle.

As a child she used to find a willow tree and would get underneath the limbs of the tree next to the tree trunk and would part the willow branches and come out and sing and perform and then go back behind her curtains of willow limbs. The only songs she knew were church songs, but she sang them from her heart to her imaginary crowd of people. God had brought her the chance to be on stage and it was truly a blessing. It was healing and helped her by doing things she hadn't done in the past.

The following year the twin brothers decided to do the show again. Janelle was much stronger now and could feel that she was nearing the end of the forest, by the light that seemed to come through the trees. The love of friends and getting acquainted once again with the family she hadn't seen for so long had been good for her. She knew she had traveled a long way on her journey to leave the dark forest so when the time came to audition for the show *Jobsong* Janelle was ready to audition for a part this time. She felt so strongly this was a part of God's plan for her. She wanted to do the part of Job's wife, as she could relate to her and the pain she must have felt losing all her children and worldly possessions. She understood how easy it would be to become discouraged and blame God, because of the pain of her loss. The part called for a sassy, jazzy blues lady, and all Janelle had ever sung was high soprano. The songs called for a low, deep, jazzy sound. No one thought she should try out for the part, because no one could see her as Job's wife. Janelle knew that this was the right part for her and she practiced the songs so she could audition. She knew it would be a lot of work and that she would have to prove not only to the ones who wrote the parts that she could do the part, but she knew she needed to prove to herself that she could do this.

She surprised everyone with the low singing voice she knew she had, but never used when she sang in church, and she got the part. She truly felt the part when she performed in that show and God let the little girl of the past who sang under the willow trees know the joys and blessings of telling His story in the Bible on stage through songs. It was very special having family and close friends of hers come to the show for some of the performances.

One of her dear friends, that she had known since she was eighteen years old, had flown to where she lived to help her during *Jobsong*. She helped her with her costumes when she would have costume changes between some of the acts of the show. It was not only fun having her there to help, but also a joy spending time with her. *Jobsong* had brought even more healing into her life and Janelle knew she was going to be all right. She was proud that she had listened to God and that she had moved toward the light in the darkness and that now she was reaping the rewards and blessings of letting God lead her out of the forest of depression and gloom.

She knew she still had some grieving to do. There were doors that she still needed to close to the past, but she knew, with God's help, the love of these new friends and encouragement and love from friends she had known for so many years, she would be okay. She knew that it was time also to sell her home. She had spent many wonderful years in that house with James, but since shortly after his death it had become her forest of darkness. At first being there was comforting, but as the time passed it began to hold too many memories of James' pain and suffering. She had got to where she dreaded going home when she would leave, because every time she walked into that house she could see him lying there in such pain and suffering so much from the seizures and all the other health problems he had lived with daily. She knew she could never begin a new life until she put some of this behind her. James would not have wanted her to remember him that way and had wanted her to sell the house when he was gone. She had never thought she would ever want to sell their home, but as time went by she knew that James had been right and she needed to sell that house and move on with her life. She wasn't sure where she would live or what the future held for her, but she knew leaving this house of pain and suffering behind was part of God's plan for her.

God brought a special friend into her life. He became a special kind of friend. He would often say things to her that she knew she needed to hear, which sometimes made her angry when he told her these things. Later she would realize that he had done this to help her move on with her life and they were things she really needed to hear. He was very kind, caring, and gentle but had the courage to be a true friend and share things with her and force her to deal with the reality of things as they are today and to not live in the past. He told her it was okay to cherish her memories of James but she had to accept the fact that James was a part of the past and she must move on with her life. That to live in the past, he told her, would be denying herself a chance to enjoy the blessings of today and she would miss the opportunities of tomorrow. He knew she had been struggling with the past and because of her deep love for James, she had found it difficult to let go of some things and move on with her own life.

James had encouraged her before he died to not grieve herself to death, to move on with life and to marry again. She had been unwilling to listen to those words when he spoke them, but knew that he had loved her enough to want her to have someone to care for her and love her when he was gone. He had that kind of unselfish love. Janelle never wanted to remarry after James' death, and was quite content to remain single and have just good friends to share things with.

They say that time heals wounds, and for Janelle time had helped. Little by little, day-by-day, the world had become a better place for Janelle. She could once again hear the birds sing, and the world had such beautiful colors as each one of the seasons would come and go. Her heart felt lighter and she could see a smile on her face when she looked into the mirror. She knew she would never forget James, but she had learned with the help of God and friends that He had sent into her life that she had been left here to do God's will and He had a purpose and reason for her to stay here and serve Him. She understood now that it had not been God's will for her to have left this earth when James did, and that God had something special in store for her. There had been so many changes in her life since James' death, but she could see now how God had been there for her during the times of changes. She also knew if she hadn't reached out to God when she did, she would be missing the joys of living for today. She would never know what God had in store for her, if she had remained depressed and forever in the forest of darkness.

Janelle never wanted to date and wasn't even looking for a husband, yet God sent this special friend into her life. He was good to call her and just let her talk and share the things she was feeling in her heart at that time. God knew what her needs were though and through their beautiful friendship God had not only opened Janelle's heart to this

SANDRA JAY KINSLOW

wonderful friend but had also opened his heart to her. She found they shared something very beautiful as friends.

Janelle was in complete denial of her real feelings for this special friend for a long time. She could not imagine ever being able to love someone again, after loving James with such depth. She had never dreamed that one day she would wake up and realize that somehow she had fallen in love with this special, dear, wonderful friend. She knew that with him she would be loved and cared for in a special way. When they both were willing to admit their feelings toward each other, Janelle knew a happiness she never thought she would ever experience again. This love for him was so different and yet so beautiful. She knew that God had brought him into her life for a purpose, and that God had opened her heart to him, knowing that he would be able to care for her and meet her needs. God had brought him into her life at the right time, and she fell on her knees in prayer, thanking God for not only being there for her in the forest and holding her hand and guiding her from the forest, but also for giving her a chance at life again. She cried and bowed her head in thanksgiving for letting her know the joys of being loved again and blessed with a future with a companion who not only loved her, but loved God as well. Janelle thought her heart would burst with happiness when they got married.

It was exciting moving into his home with him after the wedding. He had built a beautiful home up in the mountains with a view that was breathtaking. The house faced the mountains and she felt so close to God as she would sit in front of the window or outside on the deck and watch the sunrise or sunset behind the mountain. She knew she was truly where God meant for her to be. She hadn't been sure when she had decided to sell her home that she and James had lived in all those years, but she knew that selling it had been God's will. Now she had a home in the mountains with her new husband and she was thankful that God had brought him into her life and that in doing so He had brought her to a place of peace, contentment and joy. There were no demands being made of her now and she could rest and enjoy the blessings that God had brought to her. She was so glad that she had let go and let God have His way in her life. It wasn't easy to make so many changes in her life at this time in her life, but she knew it was God's will for her and she had put her trust in God and let Him lead in her life. Now she could

LOST IN A DARK FOREST

sit and look across the mountains and feel the closeness of God and see the beauty of another beautiful sunset.

When God is in charge of your life, He opens doors if you let Him, brings you joy and happiness. He didn't promise you a life of just joys, but did promise you that when the bad times come He would always be there to help you through those bad times. He did promise to bless you when you are faithful to Him and trust in Him. Janelle was glad that she had remained faithful to God. Yes, she did wonder during the darkest times if He was there. God hadn't left her; she had just been unable to reach out to Him the way she needed to. It took time for her to find the courage to walk through the darkness, not being able to see what was ahead, and do so letting God guide her when she could see nothing ahead and only feel pain. God led her into the valley and meadows beyond the forest, and into the mountains. For her it was new life, a new start, with someone very special in her life. For many it might just be the chance to travel, or do things for family or work in the church or a new job. God didn't promise the same blessings to everyone, but He will bless you according to your needs and be there for you always.

God is always there, reaching out to you and encouraging you through the Holy Spirit to let Him help you. You have to make the decision to leave the forest. Janelle will always remember the things of the past, and will always hold dear the memories of the one she loved, but now she knows the joys and blessings of having let God bring her into a world of blessings and joy. She lives for today, trusting in God for the blessings of tomorrow. She is thankful for her husband Ray, for his love and for his companionship. He is truly God's will for her. What if she had never left the forest of darkness? Let go and let God have His way in your life. The pain is still there and always will be because of the loss, but God has helped her to learn to live with it and go on with life. He has given her a new love, a different kind of love for Ray, and life once again is worth the living. Janelle never would have had Ray's love though if she had been unwilling to let go and let God lead and direct her from the forest of depression and despair. She was unsure of the future when she was in the forest, but God knew what her needs were and met those needs. You will never know what God has in store for you until you trust Him completely and let Him

SANDRA JAY KINSLOW

have His way in your life. Janelle trusted and believed in God and He brought her out of the darkness of the forest, and "yes, there is life outside the forest of darkness."

*

Printed in the United States
19566LVS00001B/98